King John and the Abbot

by

Jan Mark

Illustrated by Tony Ross

You do not need to read this page –
just get on with the book!

First published in 2006 in Great Britain by
Barrington Stoke Ltd
www.barringtonstoke.co.uk

Copyright @ 2006 Jan Mark
Illustrations @ Tony Ross

ISBN-10: 1-842993-85-2
ISBN-13: 978-1-84299-385-9

Printed in Great Britain by Bell & Bain Ltd

MEET THE AUTHOR – JAN MARK

What is your favourite animal?
The noble rat
What is your favourite boy's name?
George
What is your favourite girl's name?
Marjorie
What is your favourite food?
Pickled herring
What is your favourite music?
Klezmer
What is your favourite hobby?
Listening to music

MEET THE ILLUSTRATOR – TONY ROSS

What is your favourite animal?
A cat
What is your favourite boy's name?
Bill
What is your favourite girl's name?
Roxanne
What is your favourite food?
Lobster
What is your favourite music?
Irish
What is your favourite hobby?
Sailing

Contents

King John

The Abbot

Jack

The sheep

The dog

Chapter 1
The Abbot, the King and Jack (and the Sheep)

There are three people in this story, and some sheep. And a dog.

The first person is the Abbot of Canterbury.

The second person is Jack Shepherd. He's the hero.

The third person is King John. He's the baddy. Boo! Hiss!

King John lived in London. Jack and the Abbot lived far away from London, in Canterbury. They lived very near to each other, but they never met.

The sheep lived in a field and Jack lived in a shed at the end of the field. He looked after the sheep – that's why he was called Jack Shepherd.

There was a stone wall down one side of the field. On the other side of the wall was the Abbey of Canterbury. It was a huge house where monks lived. They were good men who worked hard and prayed to God. They lived like poor men and didn't mind getting their hands dirty.

The top monk was called the Abbot. He prayed to God but he never worked hard. He never got his hands dirty. He was very rich.

People told Jack that he looked like the Abbot. Jack didn't know if this was true because he hadn't got a mirror. But he thought it was a good joke and he liked a laugh. The Abbot was the richest man in Canterbury and Jack was the poorest.

The Abbot had servants and horses and gold and jewels. Jack had nothing but his dog – the dog that helped him look after the sheep.

Jack and the monks waved to each other over the wall. They said, "Good morning" and "Nice day, isn't it?" to each other.

Sometimes Jack saw the Abbot ride by on his fine horse. He wore silver rings on his fingers and shiny leather boots on his feet. The Abbot never waved to Jack. And Jack didn't say, "Nice day, isn't it?" to the Abbot.

Instead Jack ran to move his sheep in case they got in the Abbot's way. They weren't really Jack's sheep. They belonged to the Abbot. Jack worked for the Abbot and the Abbot paid his wages. He didn't pay him very much. In fact, Jack was the poorest man in Canterbury.

There was a gate in the stone wall. When his work was done, Jack opened the gate and went into the Abbey Church. He liked to hear the monks singing.

Sometimes the Abbot got up and talked about God and Jesus. At Christmas he told how Jesus was born in a stable. Poor shepherds came to see him. At Easter he told how Jesus was sold to his enemies for 30 silver pennies. 30 pennies was more money than Jack had ever seen in his life.

Most of the time Jack did his thinking in the field. He was on his own with the sheep and they didn't say much. He talked to his dog. The dog didn't say much either.

"The Abbot's very rich," Jack said to the dog.

The dog looked at him.

"But Jesus was a poor man like me," Jack said. "I don't think he ever had 30 silver pennies in his pocket, do you?"

The dog didn't answer.

Jack started work when the sun came up and went to bed when it set. Sometimes he thought about where the sun went at night and whether it would come back in the morning.

He thought that the sun went round the earth and he thought that the earth was flat. So did the monks. So did the Abbot. Even the King thought the earth was flat. All this happened a long time ago. In those days everyone thought the earth was flat. They thought the moon was made of cheese too.

In summer the sun rose early and set late. The days were long and warm, and Jack and his dog sat in the sunshine and watched the sheep.

"Where does the sun go at night?" Jack said to the dog.

If the dog knew the answer, it didn't tell him.

That was why Jack spent so much time thinking. He never got answers to the questions he asked.

In winter the nights were long and cold. Wind blew through holes in the shed. Rain came through holes in the roof. Jack shivered. He curled up with the dog to keep warm.

Then Jack thought of the Abbot sitting by the big fire in the Abbey. His servants were bringing him hot food and drink.

"We could do with some of that," Jack said to the dog.

Jack didn't know that someone else was thinking about the Abbot. Far away, in London, the King had heard about the Abbot of Canterbury.

King John was hopeless with money. He never had enough, and when he did have it he spent it. He was always trying to think of ways to get more.

When someone told him about the rich Abbot his eyes shone. He smiled a nasty smile. He twiddled his thumbs.

That night he thought of a cunning plan.

Chapter 2
The Abbot and the King

One evening, Jack was fetching his sheep in for the night when a man on a horse rode up to the Abbey. He seemed to be in a hurry.

Next morning, the man rode away again. A little while later Jack saw the Abbot riding across the field. The Abbot was in a hurry too and didn't notice Jack. The Abbot never did notice Jack, but this time he had a lot to think about.

Last night a man had come from London with a message. The message was from the King.

No one liked getting messages from King John. He always wanted money. Because he was King he didn't have to ask nicely. He just told people, "Give me your money." And they gave it to him.

How much money does he want from me? thought the Abbot, as he rode to London. He was worried.

It took three days to get to London. The Abbot grew more and more worried. He went to bed worried and he woke up worried.

The King knows I'm a rich man, he thought. *He'll want as much as he can get.*

When he got to London, the Abbot went to the Royal Palace. The King was waiting on his throne. The Abbot bowed low to the King. The King smiled and twiddled his thumbs.

"Well now," said King John, "so you're the Abbot of Canterbury."

"Yes, your Majesty," the Abbot said.

"I saw you come in at the gate," the King said. "You have a very fine horse."

"Would you like to keep him?" the Abbot said.

"How many horses do you have?" asked the King.

"Ten, your Majesty."

"You can keep this one. I'll have the other nine," the King said. "How many servants do you have?"

"A hundred, your Majesty," said the Abbot. He knew what was coming.

"That's rather a lot," the King said. (He had five hundred servants himself.)

"Shall I send them to you?"

"Just ninety-nine. I won't need them all. Tell me," the King went on. "Is it true that you eat off gold plates?"

"I'll have them sent to you at once," said the Abbot.

"I expect you have lots of jewels tucked away," the King said. He twiddled his thumbs again.

"You can have them all."

"All but one," the King said. "I'm not greedy. You seem to spend a lot of money. Where do you get it?"

"It's all mine," the Abbot said. "My father was a rich man." He was afraid now, not just worried. "I never spend money that isn't mine."

14

"I don't think I can trust you," the King said. "I can't trust anyone who has so much money. I think you're plotting against me. I expect you want to be King."

The Abbot fell to his knees. "Your Majesty," he said, "I'm loyal to you. To prove it I'll send you everything I own. Every jewel, every servant, every horse, every gold plate."

"And every penny," the King said. He twiddled his thumbs like mad. "But I told you. I'm not greedy. I'll give you a chance. Let's play a little game."

The Abbot started to sweat. This little game didn't sound like fun.

"We'll have a quiz," the King said. "I'll ask you three questions. If you get the answers right you can keep everything."

"What happens if I get them wrong?" the Abbot said.

"Then I'll keep everything," the King said. "Ready? Question number one. You see me sitting here on my golden throne, with my golden crown on my head. All my servants are standing round me. Tell me, how much money do you think I'm worth?"

"Can I have time to work it out?" the Abbot said. He had no idea how much the King was worth.

"I'll think about it," the King said. "Question number two. How long will it take me to ride around the earth? If I have a horse as good as yours, say. And question number three. Tell me what I'm thinking."

The Abbot banged his head on the floor. He said, "Your Majesty, those are hard questions. I may be a rich man but I'm not a clever one. Can you let me have some time to think about the answers?"

"How long do you want?" the King said, twiddling again.

"Three weeks?" the Abbot said. "One week for each question?"

"All right," King John said. "I'm in a good mood today. I'll let you have three weeks. Then you must come back here and tell me the answers."

"Can I ask a friend?" asked the Abbot.

"Ask who you like," King John answered.

"And if I get the answers wrong, will you take away everything I own?" the Abbot said.

"Everything you own and one thing more," King John said. "If you get the answer wrong I'll take away your life as well. I'll cut off your head."

Chapter 3
The Abbot All Alone

The Abbot rode away from the palace very slowly. It was a fine spring day. The sun was shining. The birds were singing, even in the middle of London. People in the streets were talking and laughing.

The Abbot didn't see them. He didn't hear the birds. He didn't feel the sunshine. He was cold and shivering.

The King has tricked me, he thought. *He knows I can't answer his three questions. I'm going to die.*

Why didn't he just take all my money and my horses and my servants and my jewels? I can't stop him. I don't mind being poor. My monks are poor men.

He's playing a game with me because he's cruel as well as greedy. He wants to make me scared.

I'm not scared of dying. If I was a soldier I'd go into battle and fight bravely. I don't mind a fair fight. But this isn't fair.

He went to a friend's house. The friend was a monk too. He was happy to see the Abbot and they sat down to talk.

"Tell me," said the Abbot. "How much do you think the King is worth?"

"Not much, if you ask me," his friend said. "But don't tell anyone I said so."

"I mean how much money has he got, if you add everything together?" the Abbot said.

"He's never got enough, I know that," said the friend.

They had a drink and talked about the weather.

"Tell me," the Abbot said. "Just as a matter of interest. How long do you think it would take to ride around the earth?"

"Years," the friend said. "I'm glad I haven't got to do it. Why do you ask?"

"Oh, I was just thinking," the Abbot said. He was ashamed to let his friend know how the King had tricked him.

They had another drink.

"By the way," the Abbot said. "What do you think the King thinks about?"

"I've no idea," said the friend. "All I know is that I try not to think about the King."

The Abbot said goodbye to his friend and rode sadly away. Perhaps he'd never see him again.

The next day he went to Oxford where many clever men lived. It took him three days to get there. He stayed four days and spoke to every clever man he met.

He asked them, "What is the King worth? How long does it take to ride around the earth? What does the King think about?"

No one could tell him.

The first week was over.

After that he went to Cambridge, to find more clever men. It took him four days to get there.

He spent three days looking for clever men to talk to. He asked them, "What is the King worth? How long does it take to ride around the earth? What does the King think about?"

And still no one could tell him the
answers. All they said was, "Why do you want
to know?"

The Abbot was still too embarrassed to
tell them.

People were very rude about King John. Some said he wasn't worth a penny. Some said he wasn't worth kicking. They knew these weren't the right answers but it made them feel better.

Even the Abbot felt better – for a few minutes.

No one really knew what the King was thinking.

"He thinks he can do what he likes," they said.

"And he's right," they said. "He does do what he likes."

"I know," said the Abbot.

No one knew how long it took to ride around the earth, but the Abbot knew that it would take him three days to get back to London.

The second week was over.

I've only got one week left now, he thought. *I won't go back to London. I'll go home to Canterbury. I can't answer the questions. I can't answer them in three years, never mind three weeks. If King John wants me he can come and get me.*

It took him four days to ride back to Canterbury.

The first morning on his way home he woke up and thought, *I've got six days left before I die. I'm sorry for any bad things I've done.*

On the second morning he was still on his way home. He thought, *I've got five days left before I die. I wish I'd been a better man, I wish I'd worked hard like my monks, and got my hands dirty.*

On the third morning he was getting nearer to Canterbury. He thought, *I've got four days left. Perhaps I can do something good before I die. I can give away my money before the King gets his hands on it.*

But on the fourth morning all he thought was, *tonight I'll be back in Canterbury. At least I'll die at home in my own Abbey.*

Chapter 4
Jack and the Abbot

Jack was in the field with the sheep when the Abbot came home.

The sun was low in the sky. The shadows were long. Jack saw the Abbot's long shadow before he saw the Abbot.

The Abbot was riding slowly. His head hung down. He looked at the ground.

"What's he looking at?" Jack said to the dog. "There's nothing to see except grass and sheep."

As he came nearer, the Abbot looked up. For the first time in his life he noticed Jack.

Jack saw how sad the Abbot looked. For the first time in his life Jack spoke to the Abbot.

"Good evening," he said.

"It's not a good evening for me," said the Abbot. "In three days time I'm going to die."

"Are you ill?" Jack said. "You look tired and sad. Come and sit by the wall. I'll go and fetch the monks to help you."

"No, I'm not ill," the Abbot said. "And no one can help me."

But he got down from his horse. He and Jack went over to the wall and sat on the grass. The dog sat beside them. The Abbot hadn't sat on the grass since he was a little boy. In the Abbey he sat on a throne that was almost as fine as the one the King sat on.

I suppose the King'll want that too, the Abbot thought.

After a bit Jack said, "Why are you going to die?"

"Because the King's going to cut off my head," the Abbot said.

After a bit Jack said, "That's bad news. Why?"

"He wants my money," the Abbot said. "He wants my money and my jewels. He wants my servants and my horses. And I expect he wants my sheep."

"Why don't you give them to him?" Jack said. "He's the King. He can take what he wants. You don't have to die."

"Yes, I do," the Abbot said. "He's playing a cruel game with me. He asked me three questions and if I can't answer every one of them, he'll cut off my head. And I don't know the answers to any of them. No one does."

Jack thought for a moment. Then he said, "What are the questions?"

The Abbot told him. "The King wants to know how much he's worth. He wants to know how long it takes to ride around the earth. And he wants me to tell him what he's thinking. No one knows what he's thinking. He changes his mind every five minutes. He's famous for that."

Jack sat and thought hard. After a bit he said, "It's all right. You don't have to die."

"Yes, I do," the Abbot said. "In three days time."

"No," said Jack. "You don't. I have a plan. Did the King see your face when you met him?"

"I bowed low and kept on bowing," the Abbot said. "You have to do that when you meet the King. I ended up flat on the floor. Anyway he wasn't looking at my face. He was looking at my fur cloak, and my jewels. He was counting my rings."

"People say I look a bit like you," Jack said. "I don't know if that's right. I've never seen my own face. But I'm as tall as you. You're fatter, that's all. This is what we'll do. You lend me your fur cloak and hat and boots. Let me wear your rings. I'll ride to London on your horse with your servants behind me. I'll go to the King and answer the questions."

"Do you know the answers?" the Abbot said. He smiled, for the first time in three weeks.

"I may be a poor shepherd but I'm not an idiot," Jack said. "Yes, I know the answers."

"Then tell them to me," the Abbot said. "And I'll go back to London this very night."

"No," Jack said. "We'll have to do this my way. There's one question that only I can answer. Trust me."

"Very well," said the Abbot. "I can see you're a good man. What's your name?"

"Jack."

"You're a good man, Jack. Tomorrow I'll give you all the things you need and you can go to London. I'll stay here and look after your sheep."

"Don't be daft," Jack said. "You'll leave the gate open and they'll all run away. You'll forget to feed my dog. Send one of your monks to look after the sheep. They know what they're doing."

The Abbot walked back to the Abbey. He led his horse along behind him.

He called me daft, the Abbot thought. *I'm a rich Abbot and he's a poor shepherd, but Jack thinks I'm daft. He doesn't trust me to look after my own sheep.*

Then he thought, *Jack's right. I don't know a thing about looking after sheep. The only thing I know how to look after is money.*

He closed the gate. The last thing he thought was, *How does Jack know the answer to those questions?*

Chapter 5
Jack and the King

Next morning Jack set off for London. He was riding the Abbot's horse and wearing the Abbot's fur cloak. The Abbot's hat was on his head. The Abbot's boots were on his feet. The Abbot's rings shone on his fingers.

When he was a little boy he used to ride on the sheep but he had never sat on a horse before. Some of the Abbot's servants rode behind him and two more rode beside him, one on each side to stop him falling off.

When they got to London they went right up to the Royal Palace. Jack left the horse with the servants, where everyone could see them. Then he went in at the front door without stopping to knock. The guards thought he must be a great man and bowed low.

This is all right, Jack thought.

He called out, "Tell King John that the Abbot of Canterbury is here! Tell him I've come to answer his questions!"

King John was sitting on his throne. When he saw the hat and fur cloak and the boots and the rings, he began to twiddle his thumbs. He stared so hard at the clothes and the rings that he never even looked at Jack's face.

Who does he think he's shouting at? said the King to himself. *That hat won't look so good when I've cut off his head.*

"Good evening to you, your Majesty," Jack said.

"I'm glad to see you got back in time," the King said. "It's three weeks to the day since I asked you my three questions."

"I'm never late," Jack said. That was true. There was nothing to be late for, out in the field with the sheep.

"And you've come to answer my questions?" the King said. He thought, *This won't take long. In ten minutes I'll cut off his head and take everything he owns. He won't know the answers, he'll just make excuses. And when he tells me what I'm thinking I'll change my mind. I'm good at that.*

"I'm ready," said Jack.

"Right," said the King, and twiddled his thumbs. "Question number one. How much am I worth?"

"Well," said Jack. "Jesus was sold to his enemies for 30 silver pennies. I don't think you're worth quite as much as he was. Let's say 29 pennies."

The King laughed.

"Is that all?" he said. But he couldn't argue. He couldn't say he was worth more than Jesus.

"All right," said the King. "Question number two. How long will it take me to ride around the earth?"

"You don't have to ride," Jack said. "You can do it on foot. It takes the sun one whole day to get right round the earth. Start in the morning when the sun rises and keep with it. Keep going all day and all night until it rises again and you can go round the earth in 24 hours too. Perhaps you'll find out where the sun goes at night. I've often thought about that."

Is that the right answer? the King thought. But he didn't know and nor did *anyone else. Still, he said to himself, it doesn't matter if it's right or not. He'll never get the last question and then I'll have his head. On a plate.*

King John gripped the arms of his throne. He bent over towards Jack. He smiled a nasty smile.

"Question number three," he said. "What am I thinking?"

Jack smiled too.

"This'll make you laugh," he said. "You're thinking that I'm the Abbot of Canterbury."

King John did not laugh, but his mouth fell open.

"Who are you then?" he said.

Jack took off the Abbot's hat. He took off the fur cloak and the boots. He took the rings from his fingers.

"Look at me," he said. "Do I look like an Abbot? I'm his poor servant, Jack Shepherd. I take care of his sheep. Well, I answered your question. Wasn't I right?"

This time King John did laugh. He laughed so hard that he started to choke. A servant had to slap him on the back.

"All right," the King said at last. "You've won. The Abbot keeps his head and his money. But I think I'll throw him out of his Abbey and make you the Abbot instead."

"No, thank you," Jack said. "I'd be no good as an Abbot. I can't read or write. But I'm fine with sheep."

"Then I'll give you the money to buy your own sheep," said the King. "Go home now and tell the Abbot that Good King John has let him off because of you. I haven't laughed so much in years."

Jack bowed low and went out to find his horse.

If that's a good King, he thought, I hope I never meet a bad one.

Chapter 6
Jack Goes Home

It took three days to get back to Canterbury, but Jack was used to riding a horse now. They got home before sunset on the third day.

Jack rode over the hill and looked down at the Abbey. He saw the monks walking about. He saw the field where his sheep were eating grass. One monk was sitting by the wall. When Jack rode into the field he saw it was the Abbot.

When the Abbot saw Jack he stood up. Then he sat down again. His legs were trembling.

Jack got off his horse and went over to him. The Abbot was pale and shivering. He started to sweat. His hands shook.

"How did you get on?" he said. "Did you see the King? Did you answer the questions?"

"I saw the King," Jack said. "I answered the questions."

"Did you get the answers right?"

"I don't know if they were right or not," Jack said. "But neither did the King. Yes, I know I got the last one right. He wanted me to tell him what he was thinking."

"How did you know what he was thinking?"

"Easy," Jack said. "He was thinking I was you! That's why I had to go and see him myself."

Then the Abbot laughed as long and hard as the King had done. But he didn't choke.

"King John sends you a message," Jack said. "He wanted to make me the Abbot of Canterbury instead of you. But I knew I'd be no good at it. So he's given me money to buy my own sheep."

"You'll need your own field to keep them in," the Abbot said. "The field next door to this one belongs to me. Would you like to have it?"

"Yes, please," Jack said.

"And I'll build you a cottage instead of that old shed," the Abbot said. "I went in there while you were away. It's full of holes and the roof leaks."

"I've noticed that," Jack said.

"I wish you'd told me about it."

"I never had the chance," Jack said. "You never knew about me until last week."

"I'm sorry about that," said the Abbot. "Please forgive me, Jack. And, please, will you go on looking after my sheep?" the Abbot asked. "I'll never find a better shepherd than you."

"I don't know about that," Jack said. "You don't pay me much."

This is amazing, thought Jack to himself. *Suddenly the Abbot's asking me to forgive him. We're talking like friends.*

The Abbot looked ashamed.

"How much do I pay you?" he said.

"Four pennies a week," Jack said.

"That's terrible!" the Abbot cried. "Well, after this, I shan't pay you at all. You saved my life. I shall give you half of everything I own!"

"I don't want half of everything you own," Jack said. "Just a bit more money will do nicely. Give the rest of the money to people who really need it. And you might try living like your monks," he added. "Try getting your hands dirty sometimes."

Jack and the Abbot walked beside the wall to the gate. There they stopped and shook hands.

"Nice day, isn't it?" said Jack, and smiled.

"I'll always be your good friend, Jack," the Abbot said. "But tell me one thing. Why did you do it? I paid you bad wages. I never spoke to you. I let you live in a leaky shed. But when I was in trouble you saved my life. Why?"

Jack thought about it.

"For a laugh," he said.

The Abbot shook his hand again. Then he opened the gate and went in to his Abbey.

"You know," he said, "you're right. You'd never be any good as an Abbot. You're much too clever."

Jack went back to his shed.

"Thanks very much," he said to the monk who was minding the sheep.

"Any time," the monk said. "I enjoyed it. It was nice and peaceful. Sheep don't say much do they?"

"I've noticed that," Jack said.

The monk walked away and Jack sat down by the dog.

"Did you miss me?" he said.

The dog looked at him. It wagged its tail but it didn't tell him the answer.

"Never mind," Jack said to his dog. "I know what you're thinking. I'm good at doing that."

Barrington Stoke would like to thank all its readers for commenting on the manuscript before publication and in particular:

Kathy Butcher	Leah Mitchell
William Coggins	Suzanna Olutela
Jordan Cowan	Ross Quinn
Fraser Flett	Evan Ritchie
Georgi Forrest	Amandeep Singh Sansoa
Kenneth Harrow	Aleisha Smart
Jake Lee	Charlotte Taylor
Sophie Legg	Emma Taylor
Kate Long	Rachel Taylor
Craig Millar	Sarah Trainer
	Melanie Yu

Become a Consultant!

Would you like to give us feedback on our titles before they are published? Contact us at the email address below – we'd love to hear from you!

info@barringtonstoke.co.uk
www.barringtonstoke.co.uk

More exciting new titles ...

Enna Hittims

by

Diana Wynne Jones

Anne Smith is sick of being sick. So she makes up stories about Enna Hittims – a brave hero, as big as Anne's finger, with a magic sword that cuts anything. It's the best game ever ... until Enna comes to life!

You can order *Enna Hittims* directly from our website at: **www.barringtonstoke.co.uk**

More exciting new titles ...

The Runaway Chair

by

Pippa Goodhart

When Aman's parents move house, they take
the house with them! All that's left is a hole in the
ground and an old chair called Shoddy. So Aman
runs away ... and Shoddy comes with him! Can
Shoddy help Aman find his way home?

You can order *The Runaway Chair* directly from our
website at: **www.barringtonstoke.co.uk.uk**